"Puñuy, puñuy ianita.

Utulitaj átun kajrin, cheyna kanaan, cheyna kanaan."

"Sleep. Sleep, little dark one . . .

The small shall be large . . . that's how it must be, how it must be."

First published in Canada, the U.S., and the U.K. by Greystone Books in 2022
Originally published in Argentina in 2018 as *La hermana menor*
Text and illustrations copyright © 2018 Pequeño editor
Translation copyright © 2022 Elisa Amado

22 23 24 25 26   5 4 3 2 1

Greystone Kids / Greystone Books Ltd.
greystonebooks.com

An Aldana Libros book

Cataloguing data available from Library and Archives Canada
ISBN 978-1-77164-875-2 (cloth)
ISBN 978-1-77164-876-9 (epub)

Jacket and text design by Diego Bianki
Printed and bound in Singapore on FSC® certified paper at COS Printers Pte Ltd
The FSC® label means that materials used for the product have been responsibly sourced.
The illustrations in this book were rendered in crayon and modified digitally.

Greystone Books gratefully acknowledges the Musqueam, Squamish, and Tsleil-Waututh peoples on whose land our Vancouver head office is located.

Greystone Books thanks the Canada Council for the Arts, the British Columbia Arts Council, the Province of British Columbia through the Book Publishing Tax Credit, and the Government of Canada for supporting our publishing activities.

Canada

The Youngest Sister

Suniyay Moreno + Mariana Chiesa
Translated by Elisa Amado

AN ALDANA LIBROS BOOK

GREYSTONE KIDS

GREYSTONE BOOKS • VANCOUVER/BERKELEY/LONDON

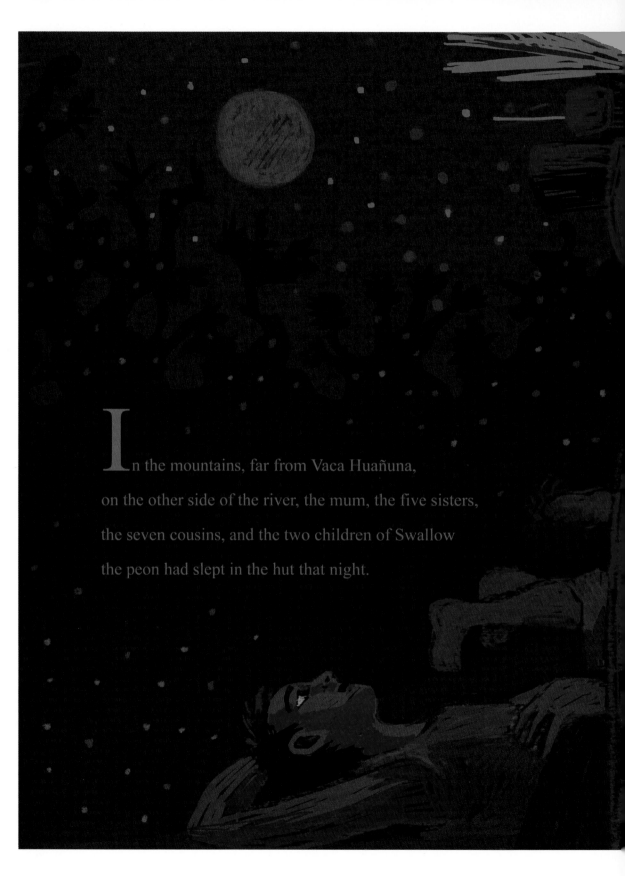

In the mountains, far from Vaca Huañuna,
on the other side of the river, the mum, the five sisters,
the seven cousins, and the two children of Swallow
the peon had slept in the hut that night.

The older ones lay on the beaten earth in the patio, sheltered from the moon. The small ones and the visitors, under the thatch. Just at dawn the mum was already waiting with the mate.

She filled the jugs and divided the cracklins with egg into fourteen more or less same-size pieces. And when they had finished eating, she assigned the tasks.

Lila got to go look for firewood.

Chiqui, to bring water.

Pelu had to search for the pumpkins that grow far from the houses but close to the river.

Noah got to grind the corn in the mortar.

And Picu—Mum sent her to get the flavor bone at Doña Ciriaca's. As Picu was the shusca—the smallest sister—she wasn't considered for more important jobs.

"I want you back before noon," warned the mum. "Don't delay in the brush."

Doña Ciriaca was a neighbor, but to get to her house Picu had to walk for two hours. Maybe a little more, or maybe a little bit less.

Who could tell, because no one there measured time with a clock. You could only know by the length of the shadows, nothing else.

Picu took the dirt road, then turned onto the narrow path. She thought she might take a shortcut through the corn, but the barking of faraway dogs made her give up on that idea.

She followed the little goat prints. There were more thorns but also more mistolas. She stopped to pick some of those reddish, sweet fruit, sucked them, and then continued along the hillside.

After walking for a while, she practiced her aim by throwing clods of dirt at the highest cactuses.

She made a slingshot out of the burlap bag the mum had given her. Then she remembered the warning and hurried on. She had to get the bone in time to put it in the pot so that it would boil a long time in the water, giving the soup some taste.

Doña Ciriaca saw Picu coming and offered her some carob seeds that she'd just cut open and some water. Picu asked for the flavor bone. Doña Ciriaca went into her hut and came out with a brilliant, shiny marrow bone. It was white because of all the times it had been boiled. She put it in the bag with a worried look on her face.

"Take it—there's hardly any substance left," said Doña Ciriaca. "They made stew with the bone in the Lemoses' hut, the Toledos', in the Juvenals', and even in the peasant Quiñónez's. So many soups . . . its taste has emptied out."

"Then, what shall I tell the mum?"

"That she should put it to boil in the soup, anyway. She doesn't need to return it."

Picu smiled. She reached for the bag and shot off with the bone over her shoulder. She heard Doña Ciriaca's voice at her back:

"Don't delay on the hillside, because the Sachajoy is about. Give the mum my best!"

icu returned to the hillside. She searched for the goat track. When she got to the white carob tree, she was feeling agitated. She climbed up barefoot, seeking the freshness of its leaves, and she chewed at a few pods. She patted the bone. Who would get it as a prize?

Surely it was Monkey Yana's turn. What with being so strong, he could easily gather up tons of squashes and pile them into a heap.

Or Chiqui's, who was the very best at finding water and lighting the fire.

Or maybe the cousins', who harvested bags of cotton as if they were all grown up.

She remembered the Christmas when they had played until dawn. Chiqui had won the flavor bone. The two of them had painted one side with mud until it was all black. Chiqui drew a goal line in the dirt with a carob branch and chose a black team and a white team. That bone was so big they had to use a stick as a lever to throw it up in the air.

"White!" yelled Chiqui when it fell on the ground with the white side up.

The black team ran around throwing things at the others and the white team ran after them.

They kicked up dust. They ran. They shouted. And they had as much fun as they usually only did at Carnival. Picu also remembered the afternoon when the bone broke into five pieces and how sad they all were without their toy. And now she was carrying a new bone!

Suddenly, a cloud of pilu-pintu butterflies flew by, very close. Picu jumped out of the tree to follow them into the brush. Like a baby goat she ran through the cactuses after the butterflies. Then a twinge in her stomach reminded her of her mission: to bring the flavor bone back for the day's meal.

She walked fast. Her back hurt from carrying the bag. The blazing midday sun heated her up so much she couldn't find the path. She searched for a long time and was sopping wet with sweat from pushing through corn stalks when she finally saw the hut.

Everyone was standing around the pot. A little smoke was rising around the iron cover like a yawn. And she could see the whip under the mum's arm.

Picu decided to hide under the amaranth bushes: not go any closer, never go back. Why should she—because, for sure, she would be punished for being late. It was always like that. She dragged herself along the ground, into the tightest bit of shade. There she stayed, very quiet. For a long time. Who knows how long?

T hen she saw her coming.

The grandmother Estanislada was walking up with her cane, a staff made from the wood of the axe-breaker tree that she used to walk straighter, to poke the fire, to kill snakes, or to make donkeys trot. She was carrying goat cheese and a bag of corn.

icu wanted to jump out and hug her. She started to drag herself out from under the amaranths when suddenly, unexpectedly, she came upon a guinea pig. It was such a trusting little animal that it was easy to throw the bag over it and trap it all at once. The flavor bone danced inside with its new companion.

Picu jumped onto the bag to get a better hold. She could feel the little creature's heartbeats as they blended with her stomach's rumbles.

And she ran out.

She crossed the field and reached the hut just in time to push into the grandmother's skirts. The mum lowered her whip to take the bag with its bone and the unexpected present.

A bit later they all drank the soup in silence. The grandmother shared the goat cheese. She brushed the hair out of Picu's face and gave her a little extra piece.

The mum put out the fire, washed the dishes with the ashes, and ordered a shorter nap than usual. Then she prepared and hung the meat in the eaves of the hut, next to the flavor bone, to air out.

W hen the sun was setting,
they gathered to eat tunas on the
beaten earth of the patio.

The five sisters, the seven cousins,
the two sons of Swallow the peon, and
the grandmother Estanislada all heard the
mum's announcement.

"Here, Picu. You have won the flavor bone."

Then she added, "For now, nothing more.
Next time, don't be so late."

Glossary

cracklins—pork rinds

mate—a traditional drink made from a plant, yerba mate, that is part of the holly family

mistolas—a fruit that grows on a cactus

peon—a hired hand

pilu-pintu—a white butterfly

Sachajoy—guardian of the woodland

tuna—a cactus fruit

Translator's Note

The text, while in Spanish, is written as though it were spoken by this Argentinean Quechua community. The translation aims to respect the very special voice in which the story is told.